Cucumber Soup

Vickie Leigh Krudwig

illustrated by Craig McFarland Brown

fulcrum kids

Library of Congress Cataloging-in-Publication Data
Krudwig, Vickie Leigh.
     Cucumber soup / Vickie Leigh Krudwig ; illustrated by Craig
McFarland Brown.
        p.   cm.
     Summary: All the insects in the garden, from ten little black ants
down to one tiny flea, get involved in moving a fallen cucumber.
Includes a recipe for cucumber soup and factual information about
the insects in the story.
     ISBN 1-55591-380-6 (hardcover)
     [1. Insects—Fiction. 2. Cucumbers—Fiction. 3. Counting.]
I. Brown, Craig McFarland, ill. II. Title.
PZ7.K9385Cu   1998
[E]—dc21   98-15679
                                    CIP
                                    AC

PRINTED AND BOUND IN HONG KONG

0 9 8 7 6 5 4 3 2 1

FULCRUM PUBLISHING
350 Indiana Street, Suite 350
Golden, Colorado 80401-5093
(800) 992-2908 • (303) 277-1623
website: www.fulcrum-resources.com
e-mail: fulcrum@fulcrum-resources.com

Early one morning in a vegetable garden, **10** little ants went out to look for food. While they were gone, something terrible happened.

A cucumber fell on their anthill and covered its entrance! No one could get in. No one could get out.

The **10** little black ants pushed and pulled. But the cucumber didn't move.

"Who will help us move this cucumber?" cried the ten little black ants.

Ants are the largest group of land insects. Most live in large nests underground. Ants are strong and can carry things that weigh much more than they do. Ants eat plants, other insects, small seeds, and crumbs that people leave behind.

"We will," said 9 noisy mosquitoes. "We will help you push."
They pushed and pulled, but the cucumber didn't move.
"Who will help us?" cried the nine noisy mosquitoes.

Mosquitoes like to live near streams, ponds, lakes, and other bodies of water. Female mosquitoes lay their eggs only in water and are the only ones that bite and buzz.

"We will," said *8* orange ladybugs. "We will help you push."
They pushed and pulled, but the cucumber didn't move.
"Who will help us?" cried the eight orange ladybugs.

Ladybugs, or ladybird beetles, are helpful insects. Farmers put thousands of them in their fields, gardens, and orchards to help keep harmful insects such as aphids and scale away.

"We will," said **7** hairy garden spiders. "We will help you push."
They pushed and pulled, but the cucumber didn't move.
"Who will help us?" cried the seven hairy garden spiders.

Garden spiders seem scary to some people, while other people think they are great helpers in the garden. Spiders will spin a silky web to catch other insects for food or to float across the garden from one plant to another.

"We will," said **6** fuzzy bumblebees. "We will help you push."
They pushed and pulled, but the cucumber didn't move.
"Who will help us?" cried the six fuzzy bumblebees.

Bumblebees collect pollen on their legs as they land on flowers looking for nectar and pollen to eat. As the bees travel from flower to flower some pollen falls off their legs, which pollinates the plant and helps it to grow flowers and vegetables.

"We will," said **5** purple butterflies. "We will help you push."
They pushed and pulled, but the cucumber didn't move.
"Who will help us?" cried the five purple butterflies.

Butterflies are gentle creatures that will often feed on the leaves of some garden plants. Some butterflies eat nectar from flowering fruit and vegetable plants and like the bumblebee, they help with the pollination of garden plants.

"We will," said 4 bright fireflies. "We will help you push."
They pushed and pulled, but the cucumber didn't move.
"Who will help us?" cried the four bright fireflies.

Fireflies, or lightning bugs, are not really flies. They are soft-bodied beetles whose abdomens glow with an eerie green light. This light is created by a chemical reaction inside their bodies.

Grasshoppers are strong flying insects that live in large numbers in fields and along roadways. They make sounds by rubbing their wings together. Farmers do not like them because they can destroy whole crops.

"We will," said **3** yellow grasshoppers. "We will help you push."
They pushed and pulled, but the cucumber didn't move.
"Who will help us?" cried the three yellow grasshoppers.

"We will," said **2** green praying mantises. "We will help you push."
They pushed and pulled, but still the cucumber didn't move.
"Who will help us?" cried the two green praying mantises.

Praying mantises fold in their forelegs, which makes them look like they are praying, as they wait for other insects to crawl by. Then they use their speed and strong forelegs to pounce on and capture their prey.

"I will," squeaked **1** tiny flea. "I will help push."

"You will help us? You're too tiny!" The other bugs began to laugh. They made fun of the tiny flea. "Go home!" they cried.

The one tiny flea ignored the others. He began to push and push and *push,* and then something wonderful happened!

Fleas are tiny wingless blood-sucking insects with hard bodies. With their long powerful legs, they can jump many times their length. They are parasites that can live on mammals, birds, and sometimes humans.

The cucumber moved!

The other bugs stopped laughing. They began to push too!

The 2 green praying mantises pushed.

The 3 yellow grasshoppers pushed.

The 4 bright fireflies pushed.

The 5 purple butterflies pushed.

The 6 fuzzy bumblebees pushed.

The 7 hairy garden spiders pushed.

The 8 orange ladybugs pushed.

The 9 noisy mosquitoes pushed.

The 10 black ants pushed

Everyone pushed and pulled the cucumber.
Soon it was off the anthill.

"We did it!" shouted the 10 black ants.
"We did it!" shouted the 9 noisy mosquitoes.
"We did it!" shouted the 8 orange ladybugs.
"We did it!" shouted the 7 hairy garden spiders.
"We did it!" shouted the 6 fuzzy bumblebees.
"We did it!" shouted the 5 purple butterflies.
"We did it!" shouted the 4 bright fireflies.
"We did it!" shouted the 3 yellow grasshoppers.
"We did it!" shouted the 2 green praying mantises.
"We did it!" shouted the 1 tiny flea.

Everyone in the garden clapped and cheered.

The little black ants were so happy, they invited everyone over for some homemade ... cucumber soup!

Recipe for Cucumber Soup

TOOLS:
sharp knife
mixing bowl
measuring cup
wooden spoon
measuring spoons
wire whisk

INGREDIENTS:
1 medium-size cucumber
8 ounces of nonfat plain yogurt
1/2 cup milk
1 tsp. dill weed
1/4 tsp. garlic salt
2 tsp. lemon juice
1/8 tsp. pepper

DIRECTIONS:
1. Wash cucumber under cold water. Peel cucumber.
2. Cut cucumber in half, then chop half of cucumber into small cubes. Set aside.
3. Mix yogurt and milk together in mixing bowl.
4. Using wire whisk, gently add in dill weed, garlic salt, lemon juic and pepper.
5. Add small cucumber cubes to mixture.
6. Refrigerate cucumber soup 1–2 hours before serving.
7. Cut remaining half of cucumber into slices to eat with your sou

Makes four 1/2-cup servings.
Serve with crackers and other fresh vegetables.

To make a great vegetable dip,
leave out the milk and let
the mixture set for one
hour before serving.